LOVE NEVER SAYS GOODBYE

written & illustrated by
STEPHANIE SLEVIN

eightfold press
LOS ANGELES

eightfold press
LOS ANGELES, CA 90049

Text & illustrations copyright © 2021 by Stephanie Slevin
www.slevindesign.com | stephanie@slevindesign.com

This book was typeset in Shrub.
The illustrations were done in watercolor and colored pencil.

First edition
ISBN 979-8-9850839-0-3 (hardcover)
ISBN 979-8-9850839-1-0 (e-book)

for my grandmothers
& my children,
forever connected

Even with ALL the people in this place we call home,

it is sometimes easy to feel separate...

ALONE.

My friend, that could not be further from the truth,
for each creature on earth is, inside, same as YOU!

Though we all look quite different, we really are linked,
inside is our spirit—
I think mine is pink!

Your spirit is made up of so many parts—
your inner **awareness**, the love in your heart.
Like a fire, it burns deep inside of your soul
so your spirit won't age, it will NEVER grow old!

It is mighty & strong
like a great LION'S
ROAR

Look deep inside, now see,
what color is yours?

My grandma's is just like the bright purple flower of her favorite spring bloom filled with

presence

&

power.

All together we live

on this beautiful earth,

full of grandmas & grandsons
from Austin to Perth!

Until comes one day

when a spirit must go,

return to its source,

back to heaven, its home.

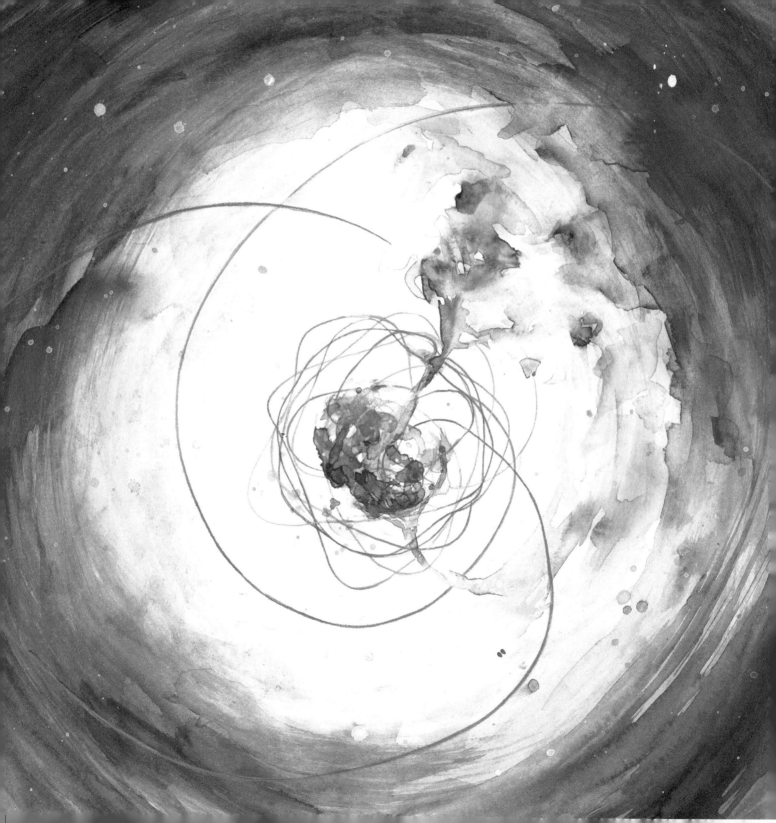

What's heaven you ask? Why a beautiful place...
you can sing or ride bikes or stuff cake in your face!

How do we get there?

However you please—ride a kite or blow dryer
or maybe a sneeze! ACHOO!

That's where grandma went

on the day that she died.

Her spirit found heaven.

I missed her

& cried.

But really my grandma did not travel far

for her spirit's still here
in the place we all are.

Did you know heaven's both in the sky & your heart?
That's where grandma is now so you're NEVER apart.

Her body is gone
but her spirit's still here.

Her energy surrounds us

so peaceful & near.

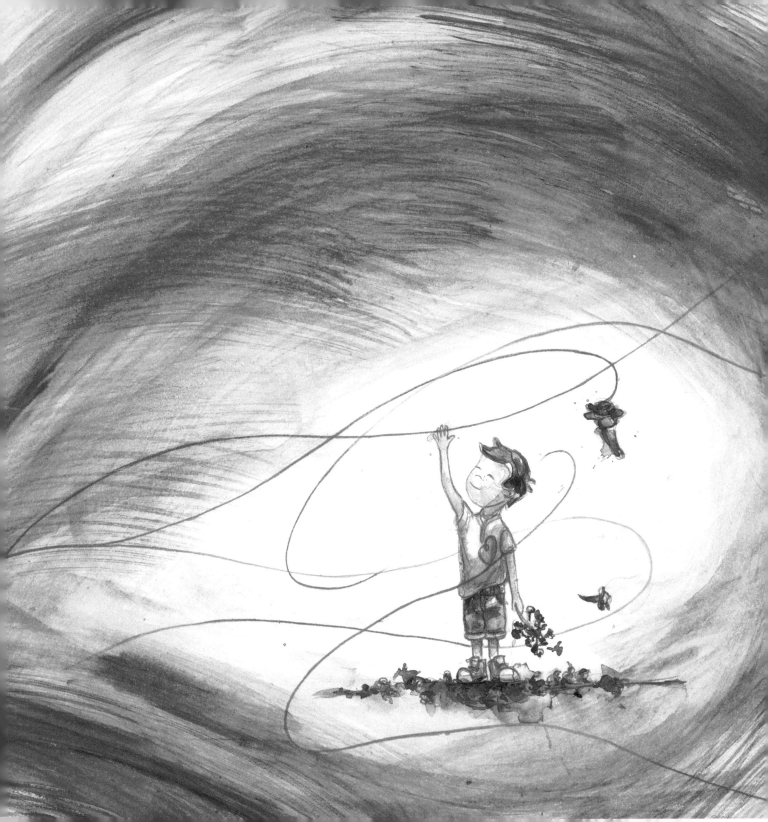

So when you miss her & feel stuck in the mud,
wrap your arms 'round yourself & just give her a hug!

Or give someone **else** a hug if you choose,
for your grandma's spirit lives **inside** of them, too.

All spirits around us, inside & above,

we are all connected,

we are all the same LOVE.

Grandma Slevin
1923 – 1991

Grandma Ebach
1931 – 2020

Author's Note

I began this book shortly after my grandmother passed away in May 2020. Both of my grandmothers had been incredibly special in my life and I struggled to support my children in their grief as I grappled with my own. They had so many questions. They were both very young and it was their first real experience with death.

I've always felt a spiritual connection to the world—not necessarily tied to only one religion—and I wondered how to convey this to them. I decided to write a book that a person of any faith could read to help a child cope with loss. I wanted to pull elements from Western belief (such as heaven existing above) as well as Eastern belief (such as heaven existing within) to create a story in which every child can find comfort. I intentionally left details in the book vague so that the parent/caregiver can elaborate as they wish: for example, choosing whether or not to discuss God.

Whether a child is dealing specifically with the death of a loved one (even a pet) or is just beginning to ask questions about what may happen when someone dies, I hope that this story in which the spirits of our loved ones live on within us, in the energy around us and through the love in our own hearts—will serve as a comforting reminder of the power of boundless love and connection.

STEPHANIE SLEVIN is an author-illustrator, graphic
designer and fine artist. This is her first children's
book. Taking inspiration from her own children, she aims to
explore spirituality in an open-ended, inclusive way that
will help kids navigate life's many ups and downs.
Originally from Austin, TX, she lives in Los Angeles, CA
with her husband, daughter and son.

Visit her at: www.slevindesign.com | @slevin.studio